I Can Read!

READING WITH HELP **2**

SPIDER SENSE®
SPIDER-MAN

Spider-Man
Versus the Green Goblin

D0006589

by Susan Hill
pictures by Andie Tong
colors by Jeremy Roberts

HARPER

An Imprint of HarperCollinsPublishers

PETER PARKER

Peter Parker is
a good student
and a loyal friend.
But he has a secret.

HARRY OSBORN

Peter's best friend
is Harry Osborn.

THE GREEN GOBLIN

The Green Goblin
is Spider-Man's
newest enemy.
He has a secret, too!

SPIDER-MAN

Harry doesn't know Peter's secret. Peter is Spider-Man!

"Harry, why weren't you at school?"
Peter Parker asked his best friend,
Harry Osborn.

"There was an accident at OsCorp, where my father works," said Harry. "Peter, my father was hurt! And now he is missing!"

Peter left Harry's house.

"I promised Harry I'd help find
his father," said Peter.

"I just didn't tell him
I'd help as Spider-Man!"

Spidey swung on a web

toward OsCorp.

But suddenly, he heard a cry.

"Help! Someone help me!"

Spider-Man saw a man

lying on the ground.

He swung down to see what happened.

"It was horrible!" cried the man.

"A creepy green guy

swooped down on a flying glider!

He hit me and stole my money!"

"In my line of work, I see a lot of
creepy green guys,"
said Spider-Man.
"Don't worry, I'll find him."

Spider-Man swung through the city,

looking for the crook.

"I'll find this green guy first.

Then I'll find Mr. Osborn,"

said Spider-Man.

Soon Spidey's spider-sense
led him to the villain.
"There's that green guy now!"
said Spider-Man.
"Hand over the money!"

The green man spun around
and flung the wallet at Spider-Man.
"Keep the change, Web-head!"
he shouted.

"I am the Green Goblin.

With my bag of gadgets,

I will take over the city!" the man yelled.

"What is this, Halloween?" said Spidey.

"Trick or treat!"
shouted the Green Goblin
as he threw pumpkin bombs.
Smoke blew out of them!

"Hey, who turned out

the lights?"

said Spider-Man.

He swung out of the smoke.

"The Goblin's smoke bomb
could only be made by OsCorp!"
Spidey said to himself.

"But what does that mean?"

"If you don't like pumpkins,

how about bats?" said the Goblin.

He sent a robot bat flying

at Spidey's face.

It ripped Spider-Man's mask.

"Oh, no!" cried Spidey.

"The Green Goblin can see my face!"

Spider-Man was angry and afraid.

He used the bat's sharp wings

to rip the Goblin's mask, too.

Spidey couldn't believe what he saw.

"Mr. Osborn?" cried Peter.

"How could you be the bad guy?"

"And how could Peter Parker

be a Super Hero?" said Mr. Osborn.

"That's a laugh!"

"It's not funny, Mr. Osborn.

Harry is worried about you!"

said Peter.

"What happened to you?"

"In the accident at OsCorp,

I was turned into the Goblin!"

said Mr. Osborn.

"I have powers I never dreamed of!"

"Don't use your powers for evil,
Mr. Osborn!" said Peter.

"Think of all the good you can do!"

"I'll leave that to you, do-gooder,"
said Mr. Osborn.
Then he pulled another
pumpkin bomb from his bag
and threw it at Spider-Man!

Spidey dove out of the smoke
and tackled the Green Goblin!
The Goblin fell to the ground
and hit his head.

"I must help Mr. Osborn,"
said Spider-Man.
"I promised Harry!"
Spider-Man hid the Goblin costume
and took Mr. Osborn to a hospital.

Later, Peter and Harry went

to the hospital together.

Peter was worried.

Would Mr. Osborn keep Peter's secret?

"Dad!" shouted Harry.

"Harry! Peter!" cried Mr. Osborn.

"What happened, Dad?" said Harry.

Mr. Osborn rubbed his head.

"I must have lost my memory
in the accident at OsCorp,"
said Mr. Osborn.
"The doctors say
Spider-Man saved me!"

"That was close!" said Peter to himself.

"My secret is safe for another day!"